We Don't Talk About That.

A novella

Emi Sano

*To all the fighters
who choose to keep fighting
and never giving up.
Thank you for staying.*

*And to those we've lost in the battle,
We miss you everyday.*

Content Warning

Be advised, this novella contains discussions of self-harm and suicide.

If you or a loved one is experiencing suicidal thoughts please contact the **National Suicide Prevention Lifeline** at **1-800-273-TALK (8255)**.

Table of Contents

MOLLY - ONE 1

KEVIN - ONE 10

MOLLY - TWO 17

KEVIN - TWO 28

MOLLY - THREE 33

KEVIN - THREE 43

MOLLY – FOUR 51

KEVIN - FOUR 62

MOLLY - FIVE 67

KEVIN - FIVE 75

MOLLY - SIX 82

KEVIN - SIX 90

MOLLY - SEVEN 101

KEVIN - SEVEN 108

MOLLY - EIGHT 113

MOLLY - NINE 117

MOLLY - EPILOGUE 124

MOLLY - ONE

He spoke to me last night and I wasn't listening. I was focused on practicing the third movement to *Bach Concerto No. 1* for my upcoming piano recital. He told me how much he was hurting and felt like no one cared for him.

I nodded, half-listening to his words as I approached the difficult mixed eighth and sixteenth notes measures. It always gave me issues and I really wanted to get it right. I couldn't really see his face as he spoke, but his voice carried softly almost like he was too embarrassed about what he wanted to tell me.

"I don't think I'm going to wake up tomorrow," Kevin said after I hit my final chord. I laughed at him, hearing him say the same words he spoke a hundred times before. He chuckled along with me.

It's just another false alarm, I thought.

"Don't worry, I'll wake you up. You're my ride to school." I knocked my shoulder with his. Kevin rolled his eyes at me as he slid off the piano bench.

"You know, you're just proving the Asian stereotype being the smart overachiever that you are." He ran his fingers through his bangs. His long dark brown hair was unkempt, showing that it hadn't been cut it in years. He grew it out of spite because of my mom. "Try to liven up a bit. I don't want to see my little sister turn into a trophy for Mom and Dad."

I stuck my tongue out at him reverting back to my five-year-old self and turned away to look back at the music. I hesitated; he was still standing nearby, hesitating as well.

"If you ever decide to really 'not wake up,' you know that would mess up mom."

"Yeah..." His voice trailed off. It almost sounded like he said, "I'm counting on it," but I just shrugged it off.

He'd made these claims before. We had been making a game out of it. I thought we had come to a silent agreement that he would never follow through. It was almost like the suicidal thoughts were a part of Kevin. They became a part of his personality.

I didn't think he was serious. I never expected to wake up to find a text message from him on my phone.

KEVIN: Liven up Molly. For me.

It was sent a few minutes ago, which was weird. Why would he be texting me this early in the morning? I was usually the one that woke him up.

I didn't understand what was going on. I had to read it over again before it came to me.

In one quick motion, I hopped out of bed, made my way out of my room as fast as I could and down the hall to Kevin's room.

It was empty, dark, and cold. He left his window open. The nights were still winter-like-temperatures cold even though it was already the middle of spring. I shut the window so my parents wouldn't freak out about the heating bill. I guess it was another way of Kevin sticking it to them.

"Kevin?" I stage whispered, my voice squeaking. I cautiously checked the closet, afraid of what monsters lay in wait inside there.

It was empty. *Thank God*, I thought to myself. Maybe I was wrong. I shivered as I worked my way out of his room. How could he sleep in the cold? It would keep me awake the whole night.

When I walked back out into the hall, I noticed the bathroom light was on. Nervous, I moved slowly towards the door, not sure what I'd find behind it.

"Kevin, you okay?" No response. I reached out and grabbed the doorknob. I closed my eyes, fearing this time that I might see something horrific. It wouldn't turn. "Kevin?"

I started to panic. Was this really happening? Was I too late?

"Kevin! Open the door, please!" *Bang. Bang. Bang.* I slammed my hand against the door. My voice was raspy and it hurt my throat to scream, but I did not want this to be real. "Kevin! Don't do this!"

I need you. My inner voice cried as I banged on the door some more.

"What going on, Hanako?" My dad's broken English reached my ears from my parents' bedroom. My dad couldn't say my name right. It sounded like "Maury" instead of "Molly" so he called me by my Japanese middle name instead. I faced him as the light turned on in the hallway.

"Dad, it's Kevin!"

My dad bolted to the door.

One. Two. Three. He kicked the door in. It swung open and there was Kevin lying on the floor. His sleep medication bottle lay on the floor beside him with a few pills leaving a scattered trail towards his body.

My dad grabbed Kevin and started feeling for a pulse. Then he looked at me with his wild sleepy eyes as he spoke hurriedly, "Call 9-1-1!"

My mom stood at the end of the hall with her hand covering her mouth. I ran past her to grab my cell phone. She struggled to say any words, but I heard her say, "Kevin, why are you doing this to us?"

I didn't say anything to her as I put my phone to my ear. I couldn't understand why she would say that.

"9-1-1, what's your emergency?" The person on the other end of the line sounded too cheerful to be a 9-1-1 operator. The whole situation of what my mom had just said and what the operator sounded like made me pause before I could speak. "Hello? Is someone there?"

"I need an ambulance. My brother overdosed on medication." The words stumbled out of my mouth.

My mom started to cry when she heard me tell the operator what happened. I watched her and wondered if she was upset because Kevin was dying or because he tried to kill himself and she'd have to explain that to everyone she knew.

I had been looking away when it came to our family's dysfunction, but it was at that moment when I finally looked at it head-on.

The ambulance came to get Kevin and whisked him away to the emergency room. We followed behind it.

The car was silent. Just as we pulled into the parking lot my mom turned to my dad and me and said, "Not a word about this to anyone."

I looked at my dad. He agreed.

I didn't.

***

They pumped Kevin's stomach to get rid of the pills he swallowed. He had been unconscious since we found him. They said that we might have caught him in time.

I didn't go to school, despite my mom's multiple pleads for me to go. I stood my ground — for Kevin. My mom and dad left for work. I stayed beside his bed.

"I should've listened to you," I said to his lifeless-looking body. "I'm sorry I laughed. Would you ever forgive me?"

I wanted to cry, not because he almost died, but because he almost left me alone with my parents. I know that sounds horrible and it was a selfish thing to say, but it was the truth.

"Don't be a trophy for Mom and Dad," he said.

It was his damn fault my life was this way. If he'd gone along with my mom's plan to become a lawyer, then I wouldn't have to pick up the slack. If he would've just passed his classes and got into a good college, then I wouldn't have to study harder to pass my honors classes. Since my mom and dad marked him as a failure, I had to become the success.

"You were so close to graduating," I tried to reason with an unsound mind. I grabbed his hand and squeezed it tightly, willing him to wake up. If he stayed longer than a few days in the Neuro Ward my parents would have to pay for it out-of-pocket. I didn't want any more blame to be put on Kevin.

I overheard my mom tell my dad to ask for extra hours at the plant before they left for work. My dad didn't look happy about it, but he agreed. He already worked ten hours overtime but his plant always liked it when he was in. My mom told me she'd be back at the hospital after she opened the store and her assistant manager came in. It was about a couple months out from prom season and she couldn't afford to close the shop.

I asked her what she told the school.

"I told them you and Kevin both came down with the flu and will be out for a day or two. You're welcome." My mom looked at me in disapproval, "I hope this Kevin thing will not interfere with your school activities and piano."

"Of course not," I told her, "I'll text my friends for chapter questions and ask them to step in for me at the Honor's Society meeting."

With that being said, my mom left happy as a clam.

I shook my head to forget that memory as I held onto Kevin's hand. With one more trying attempt to wake up my brother and snap him out of the coma, I tried to pretend we were still at home and all of this was a stupid nightmare.

"Kevin, wake up. We have to go to school."

<u>**KEVIN - ONE**</u>

"Wake up, Kevin. We're running late!" Molly's voice broke his sleep. He cracked his eyes open to see her smiling round face and bright brown eyes.

God, she's too happy, he thought to himself. He hated how happy she always was. It was mainly because he couldn't bring himself to be that happy.

"Coming," Kevin mumbled as he tried pulling himself out of bed. His body resisted with immense pain. Once again, his insomnia kept him from getting any sleep. Kevin had just gotten to shut his eyes for a few hours before Molly woke him up.

He heard Molly prance down the stairs. He couldn't help but wonder why she was always happy. How could she find happiness being in this family?

Kevin's body reacted to the hot water as he stood under the showerhead. It calmed his muscles and reminded him that he could actually feel something. But that sensation only lasted a few minutes before he went back to feeling numb. That was his indication that he needed to get out of the shower.

After the shower, Kevin opened up his pill organizer for Monday. His mom put it all together for two reasons:

1. So she knew he took them.

2. As a reminder to him that he can't waste money by skipping dosages.

When his mom put the pills in the organizer the first time she looked at him and said, "So you don't forget."

But the look she gave him meant, *this cost us fifty dollars so you better take them.*

Why did the pills have to cost so much? Kevin wondered. If they didn't work to quiet his mind, then he would've said to forget about buying them.

One pill, two pills, down the rabbit hole he goes. Moments later, reality around him slowly became a silent void and he was ready to go to school. It was like his brain was filled with cotton balls and there was a permanent fog.

He got a text message from his friend, Sarah, checking in on him.

He attempted to reply back that he was fine and he'll see her at school, but all he could get out was:

KEVIN: See you... HR

Sarah was the reason Kevin got on the pills. Her brother suffered from bipolar depression and she recognized some of the symptoms in Kevin that day he had a major schizophrenic episode in class.

Sarah saw him as he was fighting the voices in his head. Kevin dug his nails into his arm, trying not to attract attention. The voices wouldn't shut up. They were starting to overlap with the noise in the classroom. All the voices meshed together and it started to sound like when the radio would cut in and out with different stations.

Sarah and Kevin were lab partners and it was hard for her to not notice something was wrong with Kevin. He felt a flush of embarrassment wash across his face as Sarah spoke to him in a calm tone.

"Kevin, take deep breaths. Just listen to my voice. We're working on hydrogen combustibility. I can't do this by myself, so I need you to come back, okay?" Sarah didn't sound panicked. She was calm and her voice was something easy for Kevin to zero in on.

"I'm right here." She chased the voices away from Kevin and created a path for him to come back to reality. From then on, Sarah became his only friend. That's all she was to him, he insisted. She was only a friend.

Kevin apologized to Sarah after he was able to gain control of his auditory hallucinations. Sarah wasn't bothered by it at all. She actually helped validate that what Kevin was experiencing was real and he should go see someone about it. It was the first time he didn't feel alone.

Molly sat in the passenger seat of his car, finishing up the last of her vocabulary homework. Kevin glanced over at her and half smiled before looking back over the steering wheel. Her brow was furrowed as she furiously erased one of her answers. Molly always struggled in vocabulary. English wasn't her strong suit. She would much rather be nose deep in a math or science book.

"Definition?" he asked as Molly looked up at him with her mouth agape.

"Adjective. Indirect, taking the longest route?"

"Circuitous," Kevin responded without thinking. Molly's chin dropped into her chest as she wrote the answer on her packet while mumbling, "Thanks." Kevin smiled to himself; she'd never been the one to accept defeat.

As Kevin parked, he sat and watched Molly stuff her things into her backpack. She hastily threw her long brown hair up in a messy bun, just like the other girls in the school, and checked herself in the mirror. Without a word, she hopped out of the car and fled to the school like she was afraid to be seen with him. Everyone knew they were related; they were the only "Asian"-looking kids in the school.

Kevin shook his head as he started his lonesome walk to the building. Molly liked to think she fit in with the kids in their school looking the part by wearing brand-named clothes, listening to the music they liked, and dumbing it down so she was just like them.

But she didn't understand how far from the crowd she really was.

Being Japanese American was only the stepping-stone of how different they were in their school. Besides being smart, Molly was also incredibly naïve and would do anything to please anyone around her. She hated being involved in conflict and Kevin felt it was partially his fault.

Molly did her best to not be around whenever him and his parents fought. He knew that was the reason why she was always doing school activities. He wished he could do or say something to help her so she didn't always have to hide in other people's shadows.

He felt that if he removed his dark cloud from the equation, she'd finally be in the sunlight.

MOLLY - TWO

When we were younger, Kevin and I were inseparable. I was always his sidekick as we ran around the playground chasing imaginary bad guys. He sometimes would let me catch them. It didn't matter to him if I played with his friends either. I was like an extension of Kevin, a little duckling following behind its mom. He would pull pranks on me all the time, and it was always annoying because I was so gullible.

There was this one time where he had poured cola into my milk, stirred it up and told me that it was chocolate milk. I believed him, because it really looked like chocolate milk. He always wore that stupid grin on his face whenever I fell for it. And I fell for that prank three times before I finally caught on.

When I was eleven, he made me think I was late to school on a Saturday morning. I had gotten dressed so quickly and stood outside waiting for the bus for twenty minutes before my mom found out what Kevin did and called me back inside. Kevin got into so much trouble that morning because he couldn't stop laughing. I was mad at him at first, but later on we laughed about it together. We had a lot of funny memories like that.

Then high school came.

Kevin was bullied for playing the violin. We would have music lessons after school, so he would carry his case with him everywhere. The others thought he was gay or they'd make fun of his not-so-manly stature. Puberty hit late for him, and that didn't help.

The final straw was when a kid broke his $300 violin at the bus stop. Kevin just turned into a rage monster and beat the crap out of him. Dad was so mad about the violin and forced Kevin to work at the flower shop to pay it back. Kevin quit violin after that. He quit caring about school too. My smiling, happy older brother gave up on life. I never saw him again.

It felt like the change happened overnight. He woke up later than usual, refused to have breakfast with us, and stopped talking to me. I didn't understand why, until one day I overheard my parents yelling at him, asking why he wasn't more like me. He started crying.

He said, "If you want a perfect child, then start giving all your love to Molly, because I'm done. I'm done with your standards. You're right! I'm not like Molly. I can't pretend to be happy for your sake. Not anymore."

Kevin saw me as he left the living room and for the first time, I saw malice in his dark brown eyes — they almost looked black. For a split second, I was afraid.

"I'm not perfect," I said to him. He rolled his eyes and brushed past me. "I don't pretend to be happy either!" I called after him. "I like piano and I like school."

"Good for you, Moll." He continued up the stairs. He stopped at the top and turned to me. "Let me know when you start to not like it."

It gave me a bad feeling, but I let it go and continued going to practice and school. The constant struggle between my parents and Kevin carried on for a few more years, which brings us to now.

Between those times, my mom got Kevin on some medication. There were times when he got so sick from them; he couldn't get out of bed.

I watched him slowly draw into himself, and I didn't say anything about it. When another parent would ask why Kevin stopped violin, my mom would say, "He's just focusing on his studies."

I didn't understand why she'd lie, but I was told to not say a word. Just like now.

***

Nurses would come and go. I sat and waited for either Kevin to wake up or my mom to come and get me. They all gave me a detached smile as they checked his vitals. I couldn't help but feel embarrassed. I didn't want to be like my parents, but I wondered if they knew what he did.

My mom came first. She walked into the room and saw Kevin still unconscious and motioned for me to go with her. I gave Kevin's hand one final squeeze before I left his side. I was hoping he'd wake up, but I didn't really know what I'd say if he did.

The car ride home was as silent as the ride to the hospital. My mom drove with both hands on the wheel in deep concentration. I watched our small town go by as we made our way into the neighborhood. Mothers pushed their babies in strollers and fathers carried their kids on their shoulders. Everyone looked happy. They'd never know what happened to us.

My mom parked the car in the driveway and finally opened her mouth to speak.

"Molly, I know you and Kevin were close—"

"Are close," I interrupted; the look she gave me wasn't pretty.

"You and Kevin are close. But you must learn to compartmentalize what's going on. Don't lose sight from your end goal, okay?"

I nodded. This wasn't what a normal mom would say to their kid whose brother was in the hospital after attempting suicide. Then again, my mom was not normal.

She grew up in a mixed race home. Her mother was Japanese and her father was white. They lived in a small town and always made sure their appearances were well kept. Her father was a local shop owner as well and he forced them to work in the store after school. He made sure they behaved well under his watch — or else.

Then my mom met and married a Japanese man who had just immigrated to the United States, moved to another small town nearby her parents, and had two "cute Asian babies." She worried so much about how the public viewed our family because we were literally the only Asian family in the neighborhood. Our neighbors assumed we would be well-behaved and disciplined Asian children and that's how she made us appear to them outside of the house.

The inside was very different. It was constant chaos between the yelling, crying, and the arguments that never rested.

I walked into our home feeling like it wasn't my home. Kevin wasn't there and I instantly missed his presence. I never noticed how much him being around meant to me.

Even though I wasn't home often, it was assumed that he would be there. I did my best to be at home less and less; I joined clubs, volunteered for community service, and did other after school activities. He would always be around to pick me up from my activities or be sitting on the couch when I got home.

Despite all of that, knowing Kevin wasn't here...

"I'm going to check in on the shop," my mom said, her tone casual. "You should get a start on the assignments you missed today. Then later, I'll take you to piano."

I looked at her. "But I don't feel like going today."

"You are going! I paid for these classes in advance. End of discussion." My mom stormed out of the living room to our home office. I stared at the vacant spot she left behind in shock. It's like she didn't even care that Kevin was in the hospital.

I took my phone out and texted my friend Michael for class information. He sent me the list of assignments and ended the text with "Feel better" and a smiley hug emoji.

If he only knew...

As I worked on my assignments like the good little girl I was, I couldn't help but check my phone. I left Kevin's cell phone by his side in case he woke up. I knew my parents wouldn't tell me if he did. It had been almost a whole day... he should have been awake by now.

I sent him a quick message, just in case.

MOLLY: Hey, could I trade my history with your nap?

We used to have this stupid game whenever we did homework. If one of us would get bored of our homework we'd try to pawn them off on each other. Kevin always wanted to trade his math for my vocabulary assignments.

He knew I loved math and that I'd take any chance to learn something new. It took my mom a few months to realize what was happening, because I failed my tests but did well on my homework. She separated our study time after that. When we got phones, Kevin started the game up again.

"Molly! Time for piano!" My mom's booming voice broke me from my daydream. I noticed I was still looking at my phone, waiting for Kevin's reply. The cursor blinked in anticipation for me to write more. The delivered timestamp stared back at me, taunting me with its lack of "seen" confirmation. His last message mocked me. I kept staring at it. Reading it over, again.

"Let's go!" My mom called from the front door.

I quickly moved… obeying like the good girl Kevin said I was. I felt my brain fight against my muscle memory.

Liven up a little… for me.

I reached the bottom of the stairs and looked straight at my mom.

"I want to go back to the hospital, be there for when Kevin wakes up."

"No, you are going to piano. Your dad is not—"

"Dad is not here. I want to go to the hospital, now, or I'm calling Auntie Carrie to take me."

My mom gritted her teeth together. She didn't like that I was going to pull her sister into this. I knew that my mom wouldn't have told her what was going on because she didn't want the judgment to come her way.

Auntie Carrie didn't like the way my mom was raising us. She, being her younger sister, believed that we should have more freedom and live unrestricted unlike the way her and my mom did. I liked Auntie Carrie, but she also had a big mouth and would start telling the rest of the family what Kevin did, and my mom certainly couldn't allow that to happen.

"Aunt Carrie doesn't know about Kevin."

"Well, she will," I said as I crossed my arms in defiance. I felt so weird doing this. My arms were shaking; I held myself tighter. My mom and I stood face-to-face for a solid thirty seconds before she broke.

"Just for today." She turned away from me and walked out the door.

I let go of my held breath. I couldn't believe I did that. Kevin would be so proud of me.

I couldn't wait to tell him.

KEVIN - TWO

This was Kevin's last year in high school. After this, he figured he was going to move out of his toxic environment and attempt to make a better life for himself.

Sarah always pushed him to apply to colleges, even if it were a community college, just so he could get a degree. Kevin insisted that he didn't need a degree to have a content life working menial jobs. After working a year at his mom's flower shop, he'd developed enough skills to work in any department in retail. Besides, no one in a corporate setting would willingly keep employing someone with mental instability. But, she didn't believe him, and she had every right not to.

Not applying to college meant that Kevin wouldn't be making any future plans. No future plans meant he wouldn't disappoint anyone if he chose not to have a future.

Sarah knew this and that was why in homeroom she plopped down the application to a community college in the next town. Kevin forced out a laugh.

"What degree am I applying for?" Kevin asked as Sarah crossed her arms in fake annoyance.

"I don't know, English? Maybe you can be an English tutor or something."

"Like any parent would want me to be near their kid."

"You're Asian." Sarah shrugged.

"That's racist." Kevin chuckled and Sarah tried to recover.

"Just check off liberal arts. Figure it out when you get accepted."

"If—" Kevin pushed the application towards Sarah.

"When." Sarah pushed it back. She flashed her incredibly charming smile and Kevin caved.

Kevin could barely hold on to the lie that she was just his friend before attempting to respond in a normal way. Kevin really liked Sarah, but she was already dating someone. He was a really nice guy, and she deserved nice, not someone who could break her heart, like Kevin.

Besides, Kevin wasn't a douchebag who would knowingly break up a relationship just for his personal gain.

You're too soft to be a douchebag.

"So, how are you feeling?" Sarah's hard demeanor broke as she leaned in close to Kevin.

He sighed; he hated answering that question. He didn't feel anything anymore.

"Fifty percent I-don't-have-the-urge-to-kill-anyone. So that's good."

"Not killing people is generally a good sign."

Kevin cracked a smile.

Sarah tapped on his application and said, "I'm taking this straight to the post office after school."

"I can't afford the fee."

"Shut up. Just fill it out! No excuses, Kevin. I'm serious." She really meant no harm in forcing Kevin to fill out the application. But he didn't want to end up disappointing her.

Kevin spent the rest of the day slowly filling out the application. He checked off *undecided* in the list of majors.

Undecided: undecided about life, undecided about the future. It was funny when Kevin reflected on it. His parents weren't planning on Kevin's future. Sarah was. Kevin didn't know what to choose.

When Sarah met up with him at the end of the day she had her hand out expectantly.

"I didn't really write anything for the essay."

"It's community college. They don't have essays. Honestly, did you even read the application?" Sarah rolled her eyes and took the application from his hands.

"Oh, no wonder I didn't see it." Kevin shrugged and tried to smile to make light of everything. He really didn't notice there wasn't an essay section. He didn't even realize that he had finished filling it out. He remembered looking down at the end of last period and the application was filled out in his handwriting.

"See you tomorrow. Call me if you need anything, okay?" Sarah gave him a small pat on the shoulder and turned, heading to the parking lot.

Kevin watched as she walked away and wished he could talk to her more than just about his illness or planning for his future. He wanted to be able to talk about what friends talk about. He wanted to have interests like other people have.

But he wasn't like other people. Interests didn't interest him. The only things he had in his life were the voices and his hallucination.

You don't need anyone else...

... you got us.

MOLLY - THREE

I wasn't the only one texting Kevin. He had messages from someone who seemed concerned about his lack of response. I was surprised to see he had friends.

I unlocked his phone because his password was easy to crack – his birthday – and opened his messages:

SARAH: Kev, you okay? Didn't see you at school.

SARAH: Hey, your sister isn't here either... Text me!

SARAH: I'm freaking out. Please text me back.

I hesitated on whether or not I should respond. Would he get mad if I told her? Would she even have found out if he succeeded?

The three dots in a bubble popped up in the thread. I panicked. *She's sending another text*!

SARAH: I hope you're okay. You know I care about you. Jacob is worried, too. Call me.

I stared at his phone in shock. People cared for him outside our family and he still wanted it to end?

SARAH: I'm sorry about yesterday...

I wondered if this was a romance thing. Kevin might have liked her and she didn't return the love. He must have been heartbroken, but so heartbroken to kill himself? It didn't make sense.

I took her number and entered it on my phone. I didn't want to confuse her and if Kevin woke up, he'd be angry if he saw that I was on his phone.

MOLLY: Hey, this is Molly, Kevin's sister. He's in the hospital. I will let you know if anything happens... but in case my mom sees his phone, please stop texting him. She doesn't know about you.

She never responded back to me. Kevin's phone didn't receive another message. At first, I thought she was being rude, but then again, I don't know what Kevin told her about us. I wanted to know more about her, but I'm sure there was a reason why Kevin never mentioned her.

I looked at Kevin and took his hand. I noticed some marks on his forearm. I turned his arm over and saw the scars from when he cut himself.

A couple years ago, he came to me with his wrists cut up and crying for help. I didn't know what to do. I asked him why he did it; he just told me that he wanted to feel something. I remember crying with him and begging him to not do this again. He had me help him bandage his wrists up as he tried to calm down. He was lucky he didn't go too deep. I never saw that side of him before. I didn't understand at the time. I never really understood what made people hurt themselves.

I kept it quiet like he asked me. He didn't come back to me after that. But the scars on his arms showed me he had done it again since that first time.

I guess there was more he was willing to hide, even take to his grave. I started to cry. Why did we have to hide our scars from the world?

I leaned my forehead against his bed frame.

"I promise things will change, Kevin. Just come back to us."

My dad was the one to pick me up this time.

"Time to go, Hana." I looked at him through the tears in my eyes. I could see his face soften and he came to my side. He pulled me away from Kevin and hugged me close, something he rarely did. He said, "I'm sad, too."

Right there, at that moment, my dad cried – for the first time in front of me.

Here it is, Kevin: change.

***

My dad was quiet the rest of the drive home. I, too, didn't know what to say. It was a long day for the both of us. He'd always been a quiet man. He never really talked about what was on his mind. I never saw him angry, I only heard, whenever he and Kevin would get into it.

"Hanako."

I looked at my dad. The headlights flashed on his face. I looked at his tired eyes, the very same that looked scared earlier that morning. He still had scruff; he didn't have time to shave in the morning before heading into work.

"Mom is... she's processing this differently," he said. "Don't think she doesn't care."

"She is acting like nothing happened. How can you ignore your son? He's literally clinging on the end of the rope—"

"Listen. She means well. She doesn't want us to fall apart. You get it?" My dad pleaded with me to understand. I nodded to him, but I still couldn't get it. "You are still a child. You don't understand the situation. Let us deal."

When we got home, I went straight to my room and stayed there until the next morning. When I woke up, I got a text from Michael asking if my brother was okay. How did he know?

I quickly called him. "Michael, what are you talking about?"

"Have you not seen MyLife? Your brother has his own 'get well soon' page."

I put him on speaker and quickly booted up my app.

"I slept all night..." The first thing that popped up was a picture of my brother and a sappy post written by Sarah.

Kevin, we all love you. Please get well soon, and come home.

"What the actual hell?" I exclaimed. Michael chuckled a little. I rarely swear so that must have amused him.

"Who is Sarah? What's wrong with your brother?"

"I'll tell you about it at school. I'm going to need to clean up this nightmare ASAP!" I hung up and went back to the app.

"Molly?!" My mom's angry voice sent shivers down my spine. *Shit, she knows.*

I walked down the stairs and saw my mom standing there, arms crossed, visibly angered.

"Who did you tell?" I shrunk into my clothes and wrapped myself tightly. "Who?!"

"I didn't..."

"Molly Hanako Ando." That's it; she said my full name. I'm done.

"Someone was texting Kevin's phone, she seemed really worried so I told her he was in the hospital and I'd let her know if anything changed." I blurted out, so much for *not* being the good girl. My mom didn't change her position.

"She?" *Shit*. We weren't really allowed to date. Kevin was told this many times as he grew older. Dating was for adults, my parents would say. I think they just didn't want him to mess up their lives by having a pregnant girlfriend at age seventeen.

"I don't know her, I swear. I just didn't want you to see her messages and freak out like you're doing right now!"

"Do you know what you have done? You just told the whole world our private business! Now I'm getting phone calls from people asking if Kevin is okay! You just blew this whole thing wide open! We aren't ready to tell everyone.

Auntie Carrie is in hysterics. She's about to come over here and now I'm trying to convince her to stay put."

I started to cry. I don't know why. I wasn't sad, or scared, but it seemed like the right thing to do at the moment. My mom sighed and softened her demeanor.

"It's okay, we'll figure it out. Go get ready for school."

I nodded and walked back up to my room. Maybe my dad was right. This was just her way of processing Kevin's attempted suicide. My mom always needed to be in control of everything. With the whole situation being out of her control, she was trying to do anything she could to get that control back. That included controlling who knew and how our lives would be affected.

When I got to school, I walked in feeling nervous that everyone would be talking about Kevin. Michael met with me at my locker holding a giant cup of coffee for me.

Michael was your typical looking nerdy-boy: tall and lanky with no fashion sense, but still managed to look somewhat adorable. He constantly wore thick-rimmed glasses just to play up his nerd-status, but he only needed them for reading. Michael was in the same grade as me. We both bonded over how much we loved getting the chance to do extra credit in my sixth-grade algebra class. We'd been friends ever since.

"Thanks for the coffee. I needed it."

"So...?" He waited for me to speak, standing on his toes like a little boy about to get a surprise birthday present. His brown eyes widened in anticipation.

"Hold on." I took a sip of the coffee and made sure no one was close enough to hear me. There were way too many eager ears, so I moved us to the library.

"What's with all the secrecy?" he asked impatiently.

"Kevin tried to kill himself yesterday morning. He's in the hospital, recovering. He hasn't woken up yet."

Michael watched me cautiously. My hands started to shake. I put down the coffee.

"Are you okay? How are your parents?"

"Handling it their own way. Mom's super pissed about the whole situation." I tried to laugh but it came out like a whimper. "He told me, the night before... I just laughed it off."

Michael wrapped his arms around me. I propped my face against his chest, holding back my stupid tears. I couldn't believe I'd already cried twice in one day.

"You couldn't have known he'd really do it, Molly."

I pulled away from Michael and wiped away my tears.

"You want to skip?" I blurted out. "Like, go do something crazy for a change?"

"I only drove to school. My mom took the car." Michael looked embarrassed. He'd been trying to convince his mom to let him have a car since he got his license. "Besides, Mr. Jenkins has a quiz today."

"Right, maybe another time." I grabbed my coffee and we walked to homeroom together in silence.

KEVIN - THREE

Kevin forgot Molly had Honor's Society before her piano lessons after school and waited for her outside in the car for two hours with J.S. Bach violin sonatas playing from his phone. The music used to help calm his mind, but it stopped working when he started taking the medication. He still played it out of habit.

The whole time he spaced out while listening to the voices in his head. They were having a conversation about what it would look like if the school burned down.

Molly's in there, too.

"No. Not when anyone is in the school." Kevin said aloud.

But that's more fun!

Imagine the chaos...

The screams!

THE BURNING!!!

Kevin shook his head and looked at the clock. I could've been home by now, he thought.

Bored?

"Yes."

Let's go for a drive.

I'd rather just sit in the car.

Let's go somewhere far away from here.

No wait – let's just go to the park.

Kevin turned the car on and put the gear into reverse to pull out of the parking spot. Just as he backed the car out he saw Molly running towards him.

"What the heck, Kevin?" Molly screamed as she entered the car. Kevin shrugged his shoulders. He wasn't sure where he was going anyway. He turned down the music on his phone as Molly began her rant.

"Why would you take off without me? I need to get to piano. I'm late. The meeting ran over." Molly was digging through her bag looking for something.

Kevin started to move the car, but then Molly threw her hands up.

"Wait! I left my piano books in my locker. Don't go anywhere." She glared at Kevin as she hopped out of the car and ran back into the school. Kevin sat, waiting for her.

Molly was close to tears when she entered the car again. He could see the stress was wearing her down.

"Why don't you skip piano today? No sense in going for a half hour."

"Are you kidding? Drive." Molly strapped herself in and Kevin drove off.

"It's just one lesson, you could always reschedule this week."

"No," Molly sniffed back her tears, "It's gotta be today. Tomorrow I have book club and then the rest of the week is Honors Society community service."

"Jesus, Moll, why do that to yourself?" Kevin couldn't help but laugh.

"It's better than being at home doing nothing." Molly gave Kevin a look. The look that said he was a piece of shit who did nothing.

Ha! You are a piece of shit.

"I know."

After Kevin took Molly to her piano lessons, he went to Emerson Park to wait for her to be done. The flowers were trying to bloom, but the cold nights kept delaying it. Kevin plucked one of the bulbs that was dying beside the bench and stared at it. It was almost sad to look at. He crumpled it up in his fist and let it fall to the ground at his feet.

He brought a book along with him to try to read, but despite the medication, it was hard to concentrate with the voices talking in his head. During class, it was easier for Kevin to block them out because people were always talking, but at the quiet park, they were waiting for him.

Why don't you do it now?

No one will miss you.

"Because I have to take Molly home," Kevin replied aloud.

Just do it.

You've been thinking about it for a while...

... look there's the bridge.

Kevin looked over at the bridge he crossed to get to the park. He had thought about it before, but realized it wasn't high and the river wasn't deep enough. He looked down at the book in his lap and opened it.

Maybe you should get rid of Molly.

He closed his book so fast it startled a nearby bird. Kevin's fist clenched, trying to regain control. He would never hurt Molly and he knew it. But the voice was always there, telling him: *kill your sister and you can kill yourself, it's the only way.*

"No!" Kevin shouted. A jogger was passing by and jumped when he made his outburst, then quickly moved past.

Kevin grabbed his cell phone and called his therapist, but it went to voicemail. He left a message pleading for his therapist to call back. He was so close to tears.

Why weren't the pills working? He thought to himself. What else can I do to make this stop?

The chatter in his brain started overlapping. He couldn't tell which thoughts were his own and which were the voices'.

"You okay?" Molly's voice broke through.

Kevin was sitting on the bench clutching his head. He wasn't sure how long he'd been sitting like that. He didn't even realize he was clutching his head in the first place. Kevin dropped his hands and looked up at Molly. Her eyes were flickering with worry as she grasped her piano books against her chest.

"Kevin?"

"I'm fine." Kevin stood and started walking towards the car. Molly followed behind him in silence. Kevin wanted to tell her. He wanted her to know about his schizophrenia and the hallucinations. But he was afraid that she wouldn't understand. She was starting to be just like his parents, as much as he tried to make her see what *they* did, who *they* were, she had turned a blind eye to it all.

Besides, he thought to himself, we're the Andos, we don't talk about shit like that. She was never home enough to witness what they were like to him anyway. The constant looks, the comments on how he's never doing anything. It was enough to make a sane person go insane.

Molly looked at Kevin while he drove and kept hesitating on asking him a question. He could see it was killing her inside.

"I'm stressed, don't worry too much." Kevin broke the silence. He put on a fake smile, the one he'd perfected to reassure her.

"Okay, but if you need to talk…"

"Yup," Kevin said curtly.

Molly nodded and that was it. She performed her duty as a concerned sister and Kevin did his as the older brother protecting his little sister from the evils of the world – and his mind.

Kevin wanted to do more for his sister, but he knew anything he tried would end up being a disaster. He felt helpless that he couldn't be that cool older brother he used to be. He remembered being the one she'd run to if she were scared. When Molly fell at the playground when they were running away from a pretend (to her) monster, Kevin was the first person she called out for. Not their mom, it was Kevin.

But he wasn't there for her like that anymore...

She's better off without you.

<u>**MOLLY – FOUR**</u>

There's a saying somewhere that says, you know who's really got your back in a time of a crisis. After everyone found out about Kevin, no one would talk to me. My friends that I sat with at lunch and met up with for Honor's Society wouldn't even acknowledge me. It was like suicide was a disease and they were all afraid to catch it.

Michael was the only one who stuck by me. He made sure I wasn't alone. He even volunteered to recycle with me when no one else raised hands. I didn't want to do recycling at all, but I needed the hours. I was able to leave the meeting early to start and was grateful for that.

"I feel like a leper," I told Michael as I pulled garbage out from the bottle I was trying to put into the recycling bin.

"No, it's just that no one knows how to... approach you."

"It's not like *I'm* suicidal!" I exclaimed a little too loud. Ms. Carson, our AP Physics teacher, stuck her head out of the classroom. I meekly apologized and continued to finish the recycling in silence for a few minutes.

"Why are you still around? I mean I'm happy you are, but even Evy and Christina stopped talking to me."

"Because you're my only friend," Michael said softly. I stopped and looked at him.

"Shut up!"

"No. I'm serious. You are!"

"Shane, Liam, and Cody?"

"They're my fellow nerds. But we don't really talk about life problems." I started to laugh. He looked at me trying to look offended, but couldn't help but laugh along. Ms. Carson poked her head out again and shut her door. We both lowered to a giggle.

"Well, thank you. I'd rather have you than a million friends."

"Come on, Molly, let's finish this up so you can go to piano and see your brother."

Michael made me forget that I had a brother fighting for his life. It felt weird to be relieved for a few moments.

I really hoped Kevin would be awake.

As I stood outside, waiting for my mom to pick me up, I actually felt better and then I got a text from Sarah.

SARAH: We need to talk.

MOLLY: I'm listening.

SARAH: In person. Meet me @ Emerson Park 4:30? I know you have piano.

MOLLY: See you then.

My mom pulled up to the spot where I was waiting. She rolled down the window when I didn't immediately get in.

"Molly, piano lessons!" I looked up from my phone and robotically moved into the car. I was worried about what Sarah had to say. What did Kevin hide from all of us?

"Sorry," I apologized as I sat in the car.

"Had I known you two would be glued to those devices, I wouldn't have bought them." My mom shook her head. I looked at her calm and cheery demeanor. Is she still not accepting Kevin's fate?

"How's Kevin?"

"Still out. Doctors think the medicine started an effect before we found him."

"What kind of effect?" I asked, pressing her to give out more information.

"Just some chemical imbalance. Don't worry, they're working on it." She pursed her lips together. She did that when she was fighting with the words that came out of her mouth. There was something she wasn't telling me; I was going to figure it out eventually.

***

It was difficult to pay attention to piano. My teacher, Miss Meyers, was frustrated with me when I messed up the easiest measure in the whole piece. She made me stop to talk.

"What's on your mind? Clearly, it's not *Concerto No. 1*, movement three." She folded her arms across her chest. Miss Meyers was passionate about music, but very tactless when it came to small talk.

"My brother is sick," I said, lying to protect my family's private life.

"Oh? Is everything okay?"

"He's in the hospital. We thought it was the flu, but he's gotten worse. And my mom won't tell me what's wrong. I can't stop worrying about him." I looked at Miss Meyers. She didn't really move from her position.

"Well, let's find an emotion from your current state and see if we can channel that into the piece, hm?"

I was a little dumbfounded. Channel the emotions I was feeling into my piece? Okay, the current emotions that I felt were: scared, angry, sad, and lonely. The piece I was playing was supposed to be "light". I looked over at my teacher like she was insane.

"Go on, you have a half hour more of class and the music isn't going to be engraved in your memory without practice."

I faced the keys and placed my fingers on them. The cold ivory sent shivers down my spine. Was it this cold before? My fingers began playing the piece from muscle memory, but the sound it made... it was beautiful, exciting, and gave off a feeling of joy. I played my heart out and when I reached those difficult measures I was practicing when Kevin told me that he was thinking of suicide, I didn't hesitate to play. It just came out of me like a tidal wave.

For a moment, I thought I heard a violin playing an accompaniment with me. It was a harmonious sound and I imagined Kevin playing it behind me. He always had his eyes closed when he played, like he had gotten lost in the music. You would get lost in the music, too, if you heard him. That was something about Kevin I always envied. What saddened me the most when he vowed to never play again was that I'd have to live the rest of my life never hearing that sound.

We were supposed to play a piece together that year for the recital. I was practicing my hardest to catch up to his level. But when the violin was broken into pieces that plan fell apart as well. I was left playing the piano part by myself.

When I finished playing I couldn't see the sheet music because of my tears.

"That was beyond perfect." Miss Meyers' own eyes looked glossy. "There's nothing left for today, you can leave early. Go be with your brother. I hope he pulls through."

I took a look at my phone for the time. It was only 4:00 pm. I had time to run down to Emerson Park before my dad came to pick me up.

I texted my dad to let him know I'd be at the park as I waited for Sarah to show. I was really nervous about what she had to say. What could possibly be so secretive that she couldn't even tell me over the phone? Or even at school?

Sarah came right on schedule. She looked a little different than her MyLife profile, but then again, we all did. She smiled at me as she sat down on the bench.

"Hi, I'm Sarah, Kevin's friend." She emphasized the friend part like she knew what I was thinking.

"Kevin's never mentioned you before." I looked at her closely. She was really pretty, her blonde hair was done perfectly with no strand out of place, she had the best shade of light blue eye shadow on, and even her red lipstick was on point. She grimaced before speaking, but even that looked perfect. How could *she* be a *friend* to Kevin?

"Kevin told me that if something happened to him, I had to talk to you."

"About what?"

"About why."

"Because of my parents, I know that already." I leaned back on the bench feeling like this was a lost cause. She didn't have anything new to tell me.

"It wasn't that."

"What do you mean?"

"About a year ago, Kevin was hearing voices in his head. He literally freaked out in front of me. I was really scared, but I recognized the signs. He had a similar look my brother had whenever he went into his mania state. Moments later he returned back to normal. When he saw me scared, he asked what was wrong and I told him what he was doing." Sarah's eyes flit to me, seeing if I was following or panicking. "He tried to get a psychiatrist to get diagnosed," she went on, "but your mom wouldn't allow it at first. He's been battling the voices for a while now and he told me if it got any worse, or he was going to harm someone, he'd put an end to it."

I sat there, stunned. Had he heard voices in his head? I never saw his struggle except for when he contemplated suicide. But I always talked him out of it. He always lived the next morning.

"So what, he was schizophrenic or something?"

"Yes, when your mom finally let him see a psychiatrist, he was diagnosed with schizophrenia. But Kevin told me she wouldn't let him take the right amount of medication to help him because the pills cost too much. He was trying to get better, but your mom was holding his progress back." Sarah paused; she was waiting for me to respond. It was a lot to take in. Did my parents know they could have prevented this nightmare? I believed her. I could see my mom doing something like that.

"So, all the times we spoke about suicide, it was his battle?"

"Pretty much. He would text me most mornings saying, 'I won'. When he didn't text me yesterday and didn't show up to school, I was worried."

I could feel the anger rising in my chest.

"Why did you have to go public about it?" I asked, as my cheeks grew hot. Why would she blast his suicide attempt on MyLife?

"Excuse me?" She looked perplexed at why I was getting upset.

"You posted on MyLife, you made a whole page about him. What if he didn't want people to know? Did you ever think about that?"

"I... didn't."

"Yeah, well, now the whole school knows. My parents were furious with me because I told you."

"Oh, I see what this is about. You're worried about your family's image. Just like your mom."

I stood up angrily, with tears in my eyes.

"I am NOT like my mother. You know nothing about my family. You don't even know me! I don't know you. You just knew Kevin. So, don't you dare make a comment comparing me to my mother!" I stormed off and left Sarah, sitting baffled on the bench.

I didn't know what I would learn about Kevin. I expected they had a fling, but she fell in love with someone else. I didn't expect schizophrenia. I didn't think he had a constant battle in his head. I didn't know.

But my parents knew and they didn't do anything to help him and that pissed me off more than anything else.

KEVIN - FOUR

Ever since Kevin told his parents that he needed to see a psychiatrist and wanted to talk to a therapist, his dad stopped talking to him. Kevin knew it disappointed his dad. He was supposed to be the one to carry the family name into greatness. After all, that's the American Dream, right? Kevin was the only boy – man – left of the Ando family. His uncle only had a daughter. Kevin was broken and no longer brought honor. It was better for his dad to forget that Kevin existed, so he wouldn't have to be reminded of how Kevin was a failure.

Dinner was always awkward. Kevin's medicine would start to wear off by then, and his mom would only allow him to take one of the combo pills a day instead of the two he was prescribed. They increased his dosage when his hallucinations got worse, but that failed to register with Kevin's mom. Instead, she insisted on him taking his anxiety and sleeping pills, even though they made him sick to his stomach. Kevin's mom knew what was best for him because after all, she was his mom.

Kevin's hallucinations weren't some kind of cartoon bunny you see in the movies. They were like dark orbs hovering in space with little vines growing out of them. Every now and then, they would creep towards Molly, threatening to wrap her up with their vines. Kevin had to shut his eyes and wish for them to stop. The hallucinations usually disappeared if he kept his eyes shut long enough. Unfortunately, this time when he opened his eyes at dinner, they'd managed to wrap everyone.

Molly was looking at Kevin with pleading eyes; the words were barely escaping her cold blue lips, "Why?"

"No!" Kevin grabbed a knife from the table and pointed it at the black orb. Kevin's dad's voice boomed through Kevin's head and the hallucination broke.

"Kevin, what the hell are you doing?"

Kevin shook his head and noticed he had spilled his water glass all over the table. Everyone else, now free from the bindings, stared at him in shock. Kevin quickly apologized and went to his room. He quickly dialed the number for his psychiatrist. He was hoping his psychiatrist could convince his mom to let him take both the Risperdal and Zyprexa. He called his therapist, again. He needed someone to talk to, but no one would listen except the guy his parents were paying for.

Unfortunately, no one picked up.

Kevin didn't think he could stand another hallucination like that. It had never gone that bad, like scary movie bad, before.

Kevin's mom lectured him after dinner. She was frightened that he'd hurt someone.

"Why are you acting like that?" she asked him.

"I thought I saw something attacking Molly."

"There was no one! It's only us!"

"I know, Mom. I was hallucinating. I need to take more meds."

"Oh, don't blame the hallucinations, we both know it's not real."

"I don't sometimes. It feels real to me, Mom." Kevin's mom rolled her eyes and started walking out of his room.

"We are going to talk with your psychiatrist about this." She stormed out.

Hopefully, my psychiatrist gives her the answer she's looking for, Kevin thought. He was in desperate need of help. He hated feeling that way. He hated losing control.

Molly came in later on in the evening to check on him. They talked – she talked – for a while, mostly about her worries on the next recital. Kevin gave her his supportive grunts.

Molly would do this with Kevin a lot. Although, when they were younger, Kevin would talk a little more about his dreams and fears, too. But now his dreams were nightmares and fears were reality.

Molly got up from the bed and let her hands fall to her side awkwardly, "I'll wake you up tomorrow." She told him this every night.

"I don't know if I will."

"You will."

It became like a bedtime ritual. They danced around the topic of his suicidal thoughts without ever mentioning it. If Kevin had to decide between feeling like this for the rest of his life or leaving Molly alone with his condescending, egotistical parents, he wouldn't know what to choose.

> *Who are you kidding? You'd choose the latter.*

Hell, the voice was right.

MOLLY - FIVE

My Dad picked me up at the park. He gave me a "what's wrong?" look and I didn't respond.

"Meeting a friend?"

"Nope. Just collecting my thoughts." I looked out the window towards the bench I was at. Sarah had left. "Am I going to see Kevin tonight?"

"Your mom wants us home for dinner, then we go." My dad didn't sound so happy.

"Interesting," I said out loud. I wished I hadn't.

"She had already pulled the meat down for today. Didn't want to go to waste. Nothing to do about Kevin, 'kay?" My dad was getting frustrated with me. I could tell by the tone of his voice. It was the same voice he used with Kevin whenever they had their never-ending arguments.

"Sorry," I said instinctively. I was always apologizing to him, to both my parents. Sometimes, I didn't even know what I was apologizing for. It was my go-to phrase whenever I felt confrontation happening. Maybe I was making up for the lack of apologies from Kevin.

"I know you miss your brother, but he's still sleeping. Nothing to do right now."

"Okay, Dad." My voice trembled a little. Kevin was never ever in any real danger before; I had never been this close to losing someone I knew.

Mom made *gyu-don*; my dad's favorite meal. It was thinly sliced steak and onions sautéed in a blend of soy sauce, mirin, and sake with scrambled egg on top. I liked it too, but I wasn't really in an eating mood.

Not after finding out the truth about Kevin's mental illness. Not after knowing that my parents didn't do enough to help Kevin. I watched them while they focused on eating. How could they be so content with the way they handled things?

My mom looked up from her plate and I quickly looked down at mine. She sighed as she saw my barely touched food, "How did piano go?"

"Managed to hit every note and measures correctly," I responded, half-interested.

My mom wasn't amused at my lack of attention so she turned hers to my dad. They talked about work and finances. All the boring things that Kevin and I would make faces about.

When I thought about Kevin, I couldn't imagine him battling demons in his head. That couldn't be true. I wished I could talk to Kevin. I wanted to make him tell me everything he was hiding. I wanted him to know he could trust me.

"Hana." My dad looked at me, waiting for my response. I looked back confused. "We're going to leave in ten minutes to see Kevin. Eat up."

I nodded and quickly finished my plate. My mom started picking up the table. She looked more worried than usual. Maybe it was finally getting to her, or maybe she knew something that I didn't. I stopped myself from asking what was on her mind; it was just another secret being kept from me.

I picked up my plate when I finished and started putting it in the dishwasher. Out of the corner of my eye, I saw my dad consoling my mom. It was a strange sight. They barely touched each other in front of us, not even to hold hands. I quickly looked away out of embarrassment.

***

Kevin's vital machine beeped in a steady rhythm. I was pretty sure it was close to a ¾ measure, each measure had a dotted half note. Kevin would have been so annoyed to hear it. I wondered if he could.

I sat beside his bed like I always did. Mom and Dad were busy discussing things with the doctor. All I could see was the doctor's straight face as he said something to them. My mom's shoulders slumped in defeat. My dad wrapped his arm around them. Again, it was hard to watch without feeling embarrassed.

"Kevin, that's twice in one day I saw Dad hugging Mom. It's really weird to see." I watched Kevin's reaction, waited to see if he smirked in response. He didn't. Nothing happened.

I thought he was supposed to be better by now. It was just a stupid overdose and the doctors said we caught it in time. I didn't understand why he was still unconscious.

I saw somebody – not a nurse – but not a doctor either, walk up to my parents. She was wearing one of those cheap suits. The kind you wear when you have to look professional but don't get paid enough to buy the right clothes. She handed a folder to my dad, talked to him with a fake smile on her face. My dad shook his head. She nodded but insisted he kept the folder. My mom pushed away and came into the room. She looked at me with deep sad and worried eyes.

"Molly, he's not going to wake up."

I let the words hit me like a pick-up truck crashing into a fence. I didn't flinch or move away from the pain.

"I don't understand," were the words I could muster.

"The doctor said he's brain dead... no neural activity is happening. It'll only be a matter of seconds before his body gives up if we pull him off life support," she said, her voice cracking at the end. My mom, the second rock in my family broke down in tears. She collapsed in the chair near her and sobbed. It took me a full second to realize she needed comforting. I quickly scrambled to her side and wrapped my arms around her. We both cried.

Through my tears I muttered, "You're not going to do that, right?"

My mom stopped her crying quick enough to say the words that stabbed me in the gut.

"We have no choice, we have to."

I pushed away from her, suddenly filled with rage. The pain in my stomach fueled the fire.

"So you're giving up on Kevin, is that it?"

My dad walked in as I was speaking and yelled my name. I ignored him.

"He fought, years, with his mental illness to stay with us and you won't fight a week or a month? What if they could save him? What if he suddenly recovers?"

My mom looked at me like I just slapped her in the face.

"You don't understand!" she cried out. My dad stood by her side and placed his hand on her shoulder.

"You never listened to him. He asked for help so he could survive. He asked for you to help him so he could get better, but you never listened! Too worried about your stupid pride–"

"That's enough!" My dad grabbed onto my arm and pulled me away. I wrenched myself out of his grasp.

"Do you know how many times I had to talk him out of suicide? How many mornings I woke up wondering if he made it? Do you know about the cuts he made? I had to bandage him up the first time it wouldn't stop bleeding. He made me swear to never tell you. He trusted me because he couldn't trust you."

"Go. Now. I'll meet you in the waiting room," my dad ordered. I took one last look at my mom before leaving the room. It was at that moment I felt our relationship change. We were no longer Molly and Mom; I became the new Kevin.

KEVIN - FIVE

Kevin was eleven when the orbs first appeared. It always happened when his mom was nagging about him practicing his violin. They were funny because they would dance around her head and try to make Kevin laugh. As much as he loved playing violin, he hated it because of how obsessed his mom was.

Kevin missed being able to escape in the music. That was the only thing he truly enjoyed about playing, escaping the world playing J.S. Bach's *Sonata No. 1 in G minor*. He knew all four parts by heart, but loved the fourth part the best; he could play that with his eyes closed.

Violin would have been a great therapy tool for Kevin, but his mom wouldn't shut up about practicing and going to classes. That all made him want to turn away from it.

The orbs never harmed anyone, and the voices didn't start until after his mental breakdown when Kevin beat the shit out of Bryce. Everyone else thought it was because he broke Kevin's violin, but it was really what he said about Molly. He was fourteen, just about to start high school. Bryce, a year older, kept mouthing on about the "hot Asian girl" he'd like to pound one day and it didn't take Kevin long to deduce that the "Asian girl" was Molly. Kevin told Bryce to not talk about his sister, who was twelve, and he would beat Bryce up if he ever came near her. Bryce's reply was to break his violin.

Kevin's response to that was breaking Bryce's face. Bryce stayed away from Molly after that.

The other day Molly was complaining to Kevin about how none of the guys, besides

Michael, ever seemed to want to go near her. Kevin laughed because he knew it was because they were afraid of him. She didn't understand why he was laughing and just took it for one of his weird moments.

Kevin didn't know how he stopped himself from killing Bryce that day, because in his head all he kept hearing was, *Kill him!* He felt his hand break under the pressure of bashing Bryce's skull in. That's what they don't show you in the movies, you inflict as much pain on yourself as you do to the receiving person. Maybe that's why people stopped fist fighting and started using knives and guns. Only psychotic people would want to hurt themselves while hurting someone else.

Why was he thinking about that now? Why was he getting sentimental? He blinked away the past as he sat in the cafeteria during lunch. He watched another guy quickly turn another direction from where Molly sat. Would they still do that when I'm gone? Kevin thought to himself.

"Hey," Jacob, Sarah's boyfriend, sat down beside Kevin. Jacob had that perfect blonde hair and blue eyes combo that Kevin secretly envied and hated at the same time. "You okay, bro?"

Kevin looked at Jacob and nodded while smiling awkwardly. "Bro" wasn't Kevin's favorite word. He never really understood why guys called each other that. He didn't want to be someone's "bro" that he wasn't really a brother to.

"Sarah said she's not coming to lunch."

"Too bad," Kevin said dryly. He hated small talk and Jacob was the worst guy to share small talk. They were hardly alone together and when they were, it was always weird. To make matters worse, Kevin believed Jacob knew he liked Sarah.

"So, you apply to places?"

"Yeah, community colleges. Figured associate's degrees could at least get me something better than minimum wage. Which would let me move out and live on my own."

"Sarah put you up to it, didn't she?" Jacob took a bite of his sandwich and chuckled as Kevin nodded. He shook his head and started telling Kevin how he's had to apply to every school Sarah did, but here's the kicker, he didn't think he was smart enough to get in. Kevin had to listen to that the rest of the lunch period.

Meanwhile, Kevin noticed Molly tried to talk with her "friends" and be completely ignored. Michael didn't have the same lunch period, so she was stuck with the girls. Unfortunately, they weren't as smart as they were popular.

Kevin blamed himself that no one talked with Molly. He thought maybe if he did leave, that people wouldn't be so afraid of her.

She's better off without you.

"I know," Kevin said out loud causing Jacob to stop talking. He looked at Kevin, confused. Kevin quickly recovered, "I know you'll get in. You're smarter than you give yourself credit for."

"Oh, thanks, bro. I appreciate that." Jacob smiled as he bro-slapped Kevin on the shoulder. Kevin cringed inside but responded with a smile and a nod.

When lunch period ended, Kevin watched as Molly followed her friends, Evelyn and

Christina out of the cafeteria. She was a step behind them and excluded from their conversation. There's a backbone Molly was lacking in both home and social life. Kevin needed to make sure she could develop one before he left.

On the drive home from school, Kevin watched as Molly furiously texted on her phone. She groaned and shoved her phone into her bag.

"What's up?"

"It's nothing."

"Tell me. I'm bored."

"Evy wants me to do her math homework for her! I don't want to... but I don't want her to be mad at me." Molly sighed as she sunk into the seat. Kevin watched as Molly bit her lip nervously while looking out the window.

Come on Molly, develop that backbone, Kevin thought as he turned his attention to the road. He struggled to find the words to help her. This was his moment to be that good older brother.

Tell her to go jump off a bridge.

Tell her to die in a fire.

"Tell her to fuck off." Kevin shook his head, trying to regain control over his mind. He hated losing himself in front of Molly. He knew it was only a matter of time before she would catch on.

"I can't!" Molly whined as she stared out the window, "She'll hate me forever."

"Molly, do you really want to do double the homework tonight?"

Molly bit her lip and shook her head. She grabbed her phone and texted slowly. Molly placed the phone back into her bag.

"I just told her she had to do it herself and if she had any questions to just ask. Honestly, how did she get into Honor's Society if she can't even do a simple Trig assignment?"

"She probably cheated off someone weaker than you." Kevin smirked as she started to chuckle. Leaving Molly just got a lot easier.

MOLLY - SIX

My dad took a seat beside me and didn't say a word. I wasn't expecting him. We sat in silence until he handed me the folder the smiling woman gave him earlier. I opened it and saw papers for organ donations. Kevin never opted to be an organ donor when he got his license. They needed my parent's permission to take any.

I looked up at my dad.

"Scavengers."

"That's what I was thinking." My dad shook his head in disbelief. "Hanako, this is hard on all of us."

"Cut the B.S. Dad. You guys didn't get the help Kevin needed."

"We didn't know, really. How were we supposed to know? When our doctors told us 'he's just acting up, it's not mental'. How were we supposed to listen to him?"

"He was diagnosed with schizophrenia, Dad. He wasn't acting up."

"We couldn't really believe that psychiatrist. He seemed money hungry and giving out prescriptions left and right without actually giving him a way to cope." My dad shrugged his shoulders, not sure what else to say. He rubbed his eyes and sighed. My dad was tired — no, exhausted from what's been going on the past couple of days. Maybe even from the past few years. I didn't realize how much stress Kevin probably put on my dad.

I looked at him and noticed that the sides of his hair were greying a bit. I wondered when that started happening and why I hadn't noticed until now.

"Kevin never told me. I thought he trusted me, but he kept things from me, too." I felt the tears build up in my eyes. My dad put his arm around me and held me close. I felt like a little kid again and cried in my dad's arms. We sat in silence as I cried. When my tears finally dried he pulled me away so I could look at him.

"Hana, if he can't make it, the least we can do is continue someone else's life. Don't you think?"

I didn't want to agree with him. That was my brother they were organ hunting from. They were waiting for us to pull the plug on Kevin, so they could split open his body and take out everything that made Kevin human.

It made me want to scream in their faces, "This is my brother! Can't you see that? He's a person! Not just a pod!"

But my dad had a point. What was the harm in helping other people who wanted to live?

"Dad, could you wait? One more day. Just in case? Maybe he's fighting to come back. Like, I know he's brain dead, but maybe something could happen. I read somewhere coma patients can hear us and they sometimes go crazy trying to talk back."

"I admire your optimism. Don't know who you go that from. I will talk to your mom." My dad got up and left me with the folder.

I flipped through the pages, but couldn't really pay attention. The thought of losing Kevin forever killed me. I know I was being selfish for wanting to keep him alive, but who wouldn't? I just wish there were a way I could turn back the time so I could help him. I wish I could go back and drop everything to actually listen. I let him down. He was dying and it was my fault.

I failed as his sister.

I walked into Kevin's hospital room and saw my mom looking at me half upset, half tired. I could tell I hurt her with what I said. I lowered my gaze, ashamed.

"I'm sorry, Mom."

She didn't say anything, just nodded in acknowledgment. I exchanged glances with my dad and he nodded. Kevin was to stay alive for one more night. I cracked a quick smile before heading to Kevin's bedside. I placed my hand on his shoulder. I could have sworn I felt him move into my hand, but I probably imagined it.

I took my hand away from his shoulder and moved the hair away from Kevin's face. He looked so peaceful, resting on the bed. It was probably the first time he'd slept in ages.

Here's your second chance to start over, Kevin.

Please wake up.

***

We went home because mom couldn't fall asleep in the hospital room. She was too upset and needed her bed. I didn't blame her because I was starting to feel the same.

I decided to go to Kevin's bedroom to see if I could find anything, anything at all that could make me believe that Kevin wanted to live. I lay down on his bed. It smelled musty and putrid. I guess he hadn't washed his sheets for a while. I stared at the ceiling above me, something he probably did every night.

I was searching for something, a clue or a sign from him. Anything to let me know whether or not he wanted to live longer. Was I supposed to catch him in time? Was that why he sent me the text message?

I turned my head to the side and stared at his clock shining brightly in the darkness. I wondered if he felt comforted or annoyed by this light. Under his clock sat a battered looking notebook. I pulled it out, thinking this was where he would leave a note. I looked through the first few pages. They were just drawings of a dark circle with ropes coming out of it. He was so obsessive over this particular drawing. I found a few of his poems, all dark and suicidal, but no note.

If only he told me. But, he did. He tried to tell me in his own stupid way and I didn't listen to him. I was too preoccupied with my little world to realize, to even see that Kevin was going through something terrible. I could've stopped all this from happening and I would never forget that.

His last entry was just a bunch of scribbles. I couldn't really make anything from it. It looked like he did it while he was having a bad hallucination. None of these were dated. They were just a small collection of Kevin's mind.

I heard my mom cry herself to sleep. I was so selfish earlier to think that she didn't care for Kevin, that she wasn't mourning him already. I never really saw the bigger picture. Mom really did what she thought was best for Kevin.

Kevin tried, in his way, to make her understand that it wasn't what he needed. But there was bad miscommunication between them. Neither was willing to listen to each other if they weren't saying what they wanted to hear. It was like they were yelling at a mirror.

I traced my finger over the last scribble. I couldn't really see it a first, but feeling it, I realized that I could recognize the word.

Molly – he wrote my name. I looked closer at the words around it. *Fuck you. I will not hurt...*

I didn't know if those two things were related. Who wanted him to hurt me? Was this his schizophrenia?

I sat on his bed, feeling a bit anxious. I looked around me, paranoia settling in. I started understanding Kevin a little more. I picked up my phone and scrolled down to Sarah's number and called it.

"Hello?" Sarah's voice sounded like she was asleep.

"Sarah?" I started to cry. "Sarah, I need you to tell me more."

"He's gone, isn't he?" she asked, even though it sounded more like a statement.

I nodded into the phone. I cried some more. She consoled me the best she could. We agreed to meet the next day. She said she had some things Kevin gave her that might help me.

I fell asleep on Kevin's stinky bed. I didn't want to wake up either.

KEVIN - SIX

Kevin pondered if he should leave something behind to explain why he ended his life. He wasn't sure if it were a cliché to do something like that. Especially when he had a couple people in his life that would know: his therapist and Sarah. Maybe they can be my notes, he thought.

What should he tell Molly? Should he let her know that maybe this time, it was not a joke? That he really meant it? Would she believe him? Would she be the one to find him when he was dead? Would it be traumatic? Would that cause her to want to kill herself, too?

What will his parents do? Would they hold a memorial service for him? Would they spend the money to bury him? Would they even tell anyone how he died?

His mind was stuck on a speeding train without any stops. He couldn't sleep. He couldn't take a pill. His mom made sure of that.

Earlier that day, his psychiatrist called his mom and explained to her the need for Kevin to follow his prescription instructions. His mom said she would and then berated him for going behind her back. She took away his sleeping pills and told Kevin to just take anxiety and the Respiderol and Zyprexa only.

So, Kevin was awake with his anxiety levels mellowed, hallucinations subsided, but it didn't stop his thoughts. How could she hate me so much? He thought to himself. What did I do to deserve this? Why me? He was trapped in a prison cell that was his own mind. Forever forced to stay awake.

Molly "woke" him up that morning, this time with no smile on her face. If he had any energy he would ask what was the matter, but he didn't. She didn't even bounce away. Kevin wondered if he was just imagining it.

The drive to school she looked so morose, she was beginning to look like Kevin. He broke the silence.

"What's turning the gears in your brain?"

"Fine."

"Fine? That's how you answer?"

"I'm just stressed over the PSAT's next week and my upcoming recital. I also am missing a couple hours of community service and I am behind on my reading for book club."

"Oh my God, Molly, PSAT's don't count."

"I know, but it'll show me what I need to study." Molly shook her head, "You wouldn't understand, you don't care about that stuff."

Kevin shrugged. He couldn't argue with that; she was right.

"Want me to help?"

"No. I don't want to bother you."

"It's not like I've got a lot going on," Kevin muttered under his breath. But she didn't hear him, or she pretended not to.

"Kevin, what happened, the other night at dinner?"

"Stress, that's all."

"You pointed a knife at me."

"It won't happen again." Molly rolled her eyes and muttered a "whatever". She put on her ear buds to tune Kevin out. He wanted to tell her. He wanted her to know the real reason.

You tell her, you'll get locked up.

He'd rather forgo telling her. He would die before he was ever locked up in an institution that was for sure.

That afternoon he was sitting on his couch staring at the television. Molly was out doing community service and his parents were both at work. It was so quiet in the house. A commercial came on and it was so bright and loud that Kevin had to shut off the television. It left him in the darkness of silence.

He sat there for a while, so he thought. Suddenly he snapped out of his daze and found himself sitting in his car in a parking lot at

Wal-Mart. He wasn't sure how he exactly got there, but he decided to go in because he didn't want to waste the gas.

Kevin walked around aimlessly. He didn't have a clue where he was going, but after looking around he was pretty sure everyone there felt the same way. He wasn't sure how long he spent in the store, but when he walked out, after purchasing pencils, a bag of chips, some socks and a few other nonsensical things, it was dark outside. He looked at his phone for the time: it was past 7 PM.

Shit, I'm late for dinner, he thought before he darted to his car.

When he got home, dinner was already over. A plate was left for him on the table. His parents were discussing finances in the office. Molly was sprawled out in the living room doing her homework. Kevin heated up his dinner and ate in silence. It was like he was already gone and no one seemed to care.

Kevin's therapist finally called him back that evening... he said was *concerned* and wanted to meet with him the next day. But

Kevin knew that was therapist-speak for "stop calling me all the time".

The therapist's office was claustrophobic. Kevin's therapist, Colby, was cramped behind a desk with a ton of folders, pens, and papers settled on top.

Colby sighed as he sat, waiting for Kevin to begin the session. Kevin could tell he was thinking about other things.

Kevin found it ironic that whenever he came to therapy, his hallucinations and voices kept mum.

"Have you been having those thoughts again?" Colby finally spoke up.

"Sometimes."

"Have the medicines been working?"

"Sure."

"Kevin, I can't help you if you don't give me a straightforward answer."

Kevin's eyes rolled up to the ceiling. He didn't want to tell him what's been happening. He secretly wished the orbs would come and finish him there.

Kevin felt like this whole thing was going nowhere. Colby wasn't helping his symptoms;

as time went on, it was getting worse. They never resolved anything. Every time Kevin went to therapy, he would tell him what was going on, and nothing was ever suggested to help.

So, what was the point with all of this?

Colby concluded the session with the usual, "call me if you need to talk," speech. Talking didn't help him. It didn't get him anywhere.

And it wasn't like he'd ever answer the phone. It took Kevin fifteen phone calls before he finally got a response. How was he supposed to trust that Colby would answer the next one?

Kevin went to Sarah's after therapy because she wanted to give him another application she found to an online school.

He decided to ask her if she thought Molly would understand his situation.

Sarah replied at length, "Molly, from what you've told me, is too engrossed with personal issues that I feel she wouldn't really understand. You could try if you wanted, but I'm pretty sure she's had enough of your empty threats."

"Empty threats? Am I really that pathetic?"

Sarah stepped back. She shook her head as she tried to retract her words. "That's not what I meant. I-I only meant that you've shown her the signs and now she won't believe you. If you said anything to her she'd dismiss it out of hand."

"You don't know that. You don't know her."

"Kevin... you said she did nothing when you first cut yourself. She bandaged you up and you didn't get help."

"I told her not to."

"Well, what do you want, Kevin, huh? Do you want to die? Is that it? After everything I've done to help you, you just want to give up?"

Kevin sat there, feeling like a troubled schoolboy, being scolded by their principal. The anger started building up in his stomach.

"You only want me for advice, for help, which I give and then you totally disregard it! If you've already made up your mind, then why did you come here?"

Sarah's words felt like a knife just stabbed Kevin in the back. He came to the realization that she was only his friend because she pitied his situation. Kevin attempted to steady himself to his feet.

"Well," Kevin cleared his throat, "I guess I'll never bother you again."

Kevin turned to walk out of her house. Sarah tried to stop him, but Kevin's eyes were already starting to tear up, so he booked out of there as fast as he could. He heard her call his name, but he didn't stop until he reached his house. He wasn't sure how he got home or how long it took for him to get home. When he did, he went straight up the stairs and stayed in his room until his mother called for dinner.

The whole time at dinner, he sat in silence, refusing to look anywhere in case of a hallucination. Molly chatted his parents' ears off while he contemplated the best way to die.

After dinner, he hung around the living room as Molly practiced her recital piece. Kevin decided he would try to get through to her, one last time.

"Molly, can I talk for a second?" Molly stopped playing and nodded. She continued, but softly.

Kevin slowly started to explain how he had been feeling lately. He left out the crazy bits, but he tried to justify his pain. It was not physical pain he was feeling, purely psychological, but any sane person understood emotional pain hurt more. Kevin said he didn't feel like he belonged in this world and how much of a burden he was to everyone.

Molly just nodded as Kevin spilled his guts out to her. He could tell his words were falling on deaf ears. Sarah was right and he hated her for it.

"I don't think I'm going to wake up tomorrow."

Molly finished her piece and started to laugh. Their inside joke, but this time it was no joke. He chuckled along with her to make her not suspicious.

"Don't worry," she said, "I'll wake you up. You're my ride to school."

Kevin rolled his eyes. He told her to stop proving the Asian stereotype. Molly reiterated how upset mom would be. He couldn't help but feel good about that.

"I'm counting on that to happen," Kevin mumbled under his breath. Molly shrugged her shoulders and he left her side. He tried to reach out. That was his final attempt. Molly didn't need him there to protect her anymore.

She had already become *them*.

MOLLY - SEVEN

My parents signed the papers and Kevin was pulled from life support. The doctors immediately took him to surgery to harvest whatever organs they could save. I sat in the empty hospital room, feeling the same inside.

Kevin was officially gone. I no longer had a brother. I became an only child, left with parents who starved their first of affection because he didn't want to follow their plan.

It made me so angry. I wanted to tell my parents off for being so selfish. But, then I saw their faces as they came to collect me. They were inconsolable. Then I remembered they lost their son, their first child, and I felt like a complete jerk for being angry with them.

The rest of the day my mom and dad sat on the phones calling our relatives, letting them know that Kevin was gone. My mom couldn't really get the specifics out to what happened, but she insinuated that it was a suicide.

We were not practicing Buddhists. We didn't practice any religion in particular. My mom couldn't really get into the whole Christian church ideology and my dad didn't really bring his culture with him to the United States. But, my dad insisted on having Kevin cremated and we would do a special ceremony for him. He was in charge of that planning.

I snuck out of the house so I could meet up with Sarah. They were both too preoccupied to notice. Sarah picked me up and we went to a café. I didn't know why she brought us here; I guess she didn't want me to freak out like I did last time. A public place meant a smaller chance that I was going to get hysterical.

"So," Sarah reached into her bag and pulled out a CD and books, placed them on the table, and looked at me straight in the eye and said, "Kevin gave these to me one day and told me, if something should happen to him, you'll understand if you had these items."

I looked at the CD. It was a mixtape he made. It just said MIXTAPE on the CD, nothing else. I would have to listen to it to find out what was on it. The books he left were *Bridge to Terabithia* and my missing copy of *The Wizard's Dilemma* (he swore he had no idea where it was). I shook my head, but I was beginning to understand what she meant.

Bridge was the book he read to me when I was younger and eager to listen to more stories. At that point, he was reading this book for class, so it was a bonus for him. I remembered asking him through my tears why she had to die, and he told me, "Death is inevitable, it's inescapable. Death will happen eventually." His answer gave me the chills. This was the last book he ever read to me before we started to drift apart.

The Wizard's Dilemma was the fifth book in a series I actually read and gave him to read because he was no longer taking violin lessons and I figured it would be something else we could bond over. I don't think he ever finished the series. This one, the mother was sick and dying and the girl did everything she could to keep her alive. No magic in the universe was strong enough. Her mother didn't want to be saved, in the end, she knew if she managed to stay alive then every day would be just another battle to prolonging her life.

I wouldn't have been able to do anything to save Kevin, because in the end... what's one more day if you were still clinging on the edge of a cliff?

***

When I got home, I dropped off the CD and books in my room before making my way to where I left my parents. My mom and dad, still in their respective chairs, quietly stared at nothing. I sat down in one of the two empty chairs, waiting for them to say anything. I wondered if they knew I had left. They didn't really acknowledge me.

"Did you tell everyone?" I asked, breaking the silence.

My mom looked at me with blood-shot eyes and nodded. "I don't want to talk about it anymore, Molly."

"Tough, Mom, we have to talk about it. Not talking about it is what got us into this mess."

"Molly–" My mom started to speak, but my dad grabbed her hand to quiet her.

"Surprisingly, it wasn't that big of a shock to them." My dad shrugged his shoulders and shook his head. It almost looked like he was about to smile. "I think they were waiting for this since the last holiday."

Last Christmas, Kevin stormed out when Auntie Carrie pestered him about colleges. He yelled at her, "I'm not thinking that far," before he pushed past her. I have to admit, she was being a little pushy. But, the rest of the family made fun of him after that. Mom had us leave soon after.

Kevin usually hid everything so well with our extended families because he knew that's how Mom wanted it. The word "lies" was found in "families"; you never tell the truth because you don't want others knowing how imperfect your lives were. There was never any mention of Kevin's breakdowns, Mom's flower shop almost failing, and Dad getting laid off his job for three years. It wasn't something you mentioned because you'd only be putting unwanted charity and sympathy on yourself.

Dad said that after he told his brother about Kevin's suicide, his brother confessed that my aunt was actually suffering from fibromyalgia and that's why they haven't been visiting us during the holidays these past few years. She suffered her internal pain for three years without telling us about it.

"I feel guilty talking bad about her. I thought she was being cheap and not wanting to fly here to see us," my mom muttered.

"You know, Kevin did love you guys," I said after a moment of silence.

"How do you know?" My dad asked.

I shook my head. I couldn't really explain it, but I always saw him look at Dad like he was guilty. I never really asked him about it. My secret glances in his direction let me know how he was feeling that day. Normally, he'd be stoic and had a permanent scowl sewn on his lips. Sometimes, he'd be smiling and happy, those days were the best because we'd actually have decent conversations without him getting weird. When he'd look at my parents, it was like his eyes softened and the scowl turned more into a frown like he was sad.

I started to feel like this was heading into an awkward conversation. I didn't want to speak for Kevin because really, I didn't know how he felt. Maybe he did want to hurt them. I'll never know because he took that secret to his grave. All I knew was why he wanted to die.

Because being alive was like death.

KEVIN - SEVEN

That voice, the clearest one I hear,
It beckons me into the void.
Tomorrow is what I most fear –
That it will have taken over.
For if that day should come,
And my voice is no longer there.
I'd hope that maybe some,
Would recognize and try to find me.
Until then I will remain,
Hidden in the void.
One day it will explain,
Where I was destroyed.

Kevin wrote the poem for class. His teacher nearly framed it for her room. She said it was the most thought-provoking poem a student had ever written. He didn't think she fully understood it though. If she did, doctors would have carried him away in a straightjacket.

He wrote a few more because of his insomnia, but they blatantly talked about his suicidal thoughts and he was, for sure, afraid she would tell his mom.

It's funny how many times a person could reach out and try to grab onto anyone who would pull them out of the water yet still, find themselves drowning. Kevin felt like he was in the middle of the ocean on a capsized boat, screaming until his voice started to bleed and he had lost all hope. Then someone came along, he was so happy to be finally saved and be on land, but instead, they just threw a lifesaver at him and drove away.

Kevin sat on his bed crying because he felt too afraid to do it, but he was more afraid of living one more day. One more day of his parents' disappointed looks. One more day of Sarah's pity, and one more day of fighting hallucinations and voices off from killing Molly. He couldn't survive on that lifesaver, not when sharks were already surrounding him.

Sarah's text messages kept coming through on his phone. She was trying to apologize for what she said to him. She tried calling a couple times but Kevin ignored all her attempts. Eventually they stopped.

Kevin couldn't stop crying long enough to even respond.

He cried so hard that he needed to vomit, so he ran to the bathroom and heaved into the toilet. This was the most difficult decision he would ever have to make.

As he looked into the mirror he saw his sad excuse of a reflection. Black circles sunk heavily under his eyes. He saw his hair was a matted mess – and the orbs. They were dancing above his head; just like they did the first time he saw them. It almost seemed like they were smiling. He wasn't sure how he could tell, but he could. One of the orbs was hovering by the linen closet and beckoned Kevin to open it. He opened the door and there it was: his goddamn sleeping pills hiding in between the towels. He couldn't believe it.

Take them, all of them.

Yes.

All.

Of.

Them.

Kevin's stomach wasn't in knots anymore. He never felt so sure in his life. He grabbed his cellphone and texted Molly. Kevin knew she wouldn't hear her phone go off. He just wanted to leave her with something from him in case Sarah chickened out on her deal.

Are you ready?

He's going to chicken out.

He opened the bottle of sleeping pills and poured some into his hand. He heard some movement in the hall. Did he wake up Molly? Kevin panicked and quickly locked the door before shoving a handful of the pills into his mouth. It took him a few seconds to swallow. The phrase came to mind as he struggled; they were literally tough pills to swallow.

His body's instant reaction was to gag.

Are you going to give up?

No, I'm doing this. He thought to himself and forced himself to swallow. The pill bottle slipped out of his hand.

Not too late...

I'm doing this. Kevin resisted the urge to puke. He was trying to convince himself to not back out as his body started to feel funny. The pills sudden reaction was startling. How come it never took this quickly before?

I'm doing this, he said one final time to himself as his body fell to the floor. Everything was becoming blurry to him. Kevin heard footsteps come up to the door.

And then he found the one thing he was looking for this whole time, silence.

MOLLY - EIGHT

The first song on the mixtape was "The Middle" by Jimmy Eat World and then afterward, it was just a bunch of other songs with similar meaning. *It's going to be okay.*

I never knew how much he cared about me. I always thought he hated me. He used to tell me off for being such a "good girl" and being a stereotypical Asian American, which I have to admit, I was. He used to glare at me whenever I made the honor roll or aced another test. Kevin would remind me how much he hated that he had to drive me everywhere. He would always make fun of how I hung out with friends that didn't even like me.

It really hurt me, how many faults he'd find about me. It made me hate him. It made me wish I never had a brother. I couldn't wait until he went off to college and moved out so I didn't have to hear him make fun of me again.

I kept thinking he'd walk by my room any moment and comment on my choice of study music while simultaneously laughing as he made his way downstairs.

He cared about me.

I cried while listening through every single song on that mixtape. I couldn't believe how much relief I was starting to feel. With every last teardrop falling from my eyes I was feeling a weight being lifted off my chest. It was like he knew I'd somehow blame myself for not being there, for not stopping him. In his death, Kevin was still being a big brother comforting his little sister. It was definitely something that I needed to be able to get over losing him the way I did.

Kevin was going to be cremated at the end of the week, the traditional funeral ceremony was happening the day after, and Mom had entrusted me in finding classmates to come and say their goodbyes. I told her Kevin didn't really have a lot of friends, but she insisted that he deserved a crowd.

So, I went to school the next day and found Sarah. She was sitting with a guy, who was comforting her; I assumed he was her boyfriend. We locked eyes, hers were bloodshot and tear-filled, mine were dry but tender.

"So, Kevin's funeral ceremony is happening this weekend. My mom wants you to come."

"I'm sorry, did I just hear you guys are having a ceremony?" Sarah asked, surprised.

"It's Japanese custom. I don't really know a lot about it. My dad insisted on having the ceremony and my mom insisted on Kevin having a crowd to witness him off into the 'spirit world' or something like that. Anyway, could you maybe convince some of your classmates? I'll text you the details when I get it."

Sarah nodded in response. She was in as much of a shock as I was when my parents first mentioned it. This was by far the exact opposite of what Kevin would have imagined his funeral to be like. He probably thought they'd keep it quiet because of how he died.

But, Mama and Papa Ando surprised everyone.

MOLLY - NINE

Sarah managed to get half the senior class to come to Kevin's ceremony. Out of all the friends I thought I had, Michael was the only one who showed up. My mom was impressed that we were even friends. Apparently, she knew his parents and was told that he was a contender for Harvard. Since I was too, she naturally thought we were rivals.

Most of the kids who showed up were just there to write about it on MyLife.

"How sad! I never knew he was bullied." I heard someone say. I wanted to wring their neck and yell at them for not knowing the real reason why Kevin killed himself. Sarah saw me and grabbed me before I had a chance to confront the idiot.

"Most of the people are here because it's our senior year and they feel devastated that we lost someone. Don't listen to what they think happened. You know, and that's all that matters."

"They need to know that he was sick."

"I agree, but mental illness is a touchy subject. It'll just get romanticized and I know how much Kevin hated it. Just let it go."

"So, don't talk about it?" I looked at Sarah and crossed my arms in front of my chest. She smirked in response.

"Touché. I understand. If you want to make a difference, for Kevin, be the help he needed."

I felt the heat rise in my cheeks. Who was she to tell me all of this? At least her brother was still alive. She gets to see him every day. He gets to grow old and be her kids' uncle!

"Why did you say you were sorry?"

Sarah looked at me, perplexed. I wasn't sure if she was faking it or if she was really that dense.

"Why did you text Kevin you were sorry about the night before he killed himself?"

Sarah shrunk about two inches. She burst into tears. It was so sudden that the people next to us jumped. "We got into this fight... I told him off for constantly asking for advice and not taking anything I gave. I told him how annoying it was that he'd talk about killing himself and he would chicken out. OH, MOLLY! It's all my fault!"

Sarah buried her head in her hands. She was hardcore sobbing, and I didn't know how to handle that. Her boyfriend made his way over as soon as he noticed and wrapped her in his arms. I wanted to say something to her, but I couldn't. Suddenly, I felt angry. It was her fault. If she hadn't said that... Kevin would've still been here. He'd still be fighting his battles and I'd still have my older brother.

I took a deep breath to assess the situation. What Kevin did was ultimately his decision. No one really drove him to do anything. He decided to kill himself. He decided that this life wasn't good enough for him. There was nothing Sarah or I could have done to prevent it from happening.

"We can't keep blaming ourselves for what Kevin did," I said before walking away. Sarah called out to me; I stopped and turned to face her.

"Thank you, for saying that. But, really, you should know he did everything he could to make sure you'd be okay." I believed her. Sarah was ushered away by her boyfriend and I found my way back to my parents.

I had never sat through a Japanese funeral. My dad seemed like he'd never done so either. We sat awkwardly in front of the crowd beside an old black and white photograph of Kevin in a black frame. It was a photo that he took before he grew out his hair. My mom insisted on having this photo so we'd remember his good times.

There was burning incense sitting in front of him. The incense smell tickled the inside of my nose. I almost wanted to laugh thinking how Kevin would've reacted seeing his face blown up like that. My dad handed me something that looked like rosary beads and told me to hold them around my hands as we prayed.

My aunt and uncle from Japan flew in and started the ritual. They came up to my parents, bowed and handed them a black envelope. I later found out it was money to help pay for the ceremony and final expenses. I guess that was part of the tradition so the family of the deceased wasn't burdened any more than they already were. My dad handed the envelope to my mother to keep track of. Her hands were shaking as my aunt and uncle continued to pray in front of Kevin's picture.

It was like I was watching a movie in slow motion. Everything they did was picturesque. My uncle picked up some of the incense ashes from the receptacle to the right of the incense, brought the ashes up to his forehead and then placed them in the incense burner holder. My uncle continued the prayer in front of Kevin's picture and then turned to face my dad, bowed, and walked away. My cousin followed suit and so did the rest of the family.

Although they had several people show the example of how to do the ritual, the senior class just walked up to my parents and said how much they'll miss Kevin. They said how sorry they were to see him gone. I could see my mom grit her teeth together as they spoke. She knew they were faking it.

My dad wasn't angry at their lack of decorum; we were bridging two cultures together and this was bound to happen. He wanted to make sure Kevin knew that we loved him and he wasn't in trouble. Although he wasn't religious, my dad was deeply superstitious, and he wasn't going to chance that Kevin was going to be an unrested soul. My dad told me that he wanted Kevin to know that neither he nor my mom was mad at him for what he did and for him to not worry about us.

My dad said a few prayers in Japanese, which fell on many deaf ears in the room including mine, and ended the ceremony.

When the high school kids left, the rest of the family stayed behind. For the first time, it actually felt like we were a family. We talked freely amongst ourselves. I actually had the chance to talk with my cousin who was about the same age as me. We never really said anything besides the usual "how's school" and "how's music" questions. We bonded over how awkward this whole situation was and how she never knew Kevin to be hurting like that. I tried to explain the situation, but it was hard because I never really understood.

After the funeral, my mom must have vowed to become more involved in my life. She kept asking me about Michael. It was almost comical. I told her we were merely friends and I saw him only as that. Later, I told Michael about what my mother was asking and he nearly fell off his chair in laughter saying that he only saw me as a sister.

She continued to be more present in my life as a confidant instead of being the authoritarian figure. She was doing this for Kevin.

MOLLY - EPILOGUE

Camden sat in his chair across from mine fiddling with the zipper on his sweater. He was fifteen years old and having a bad week. His parents actually dragged him in. They said that something was bothering him, he wouldn't talk to them, and there was nowhere else to turn.

I waited patiently for him to talk to me. I didn't want to push him if he wasn't ready. We already set up extra appointments just in case.

I knew that if I were to reach Camden that it would probably take time and patience.

"I'm just so anxious all the time and it keeps me on edge and then all of a sudden I'm depressed," he said softly, not looking up at me at first. I caught his eye and nodded for him to continue. "I just want to be able to sleep. I'm so tired. Even when I'm not anxious. I just want to take a whole ton of sleeping pills so I can get some sleep. Am I messed up?"

I shook my head, "No, don't ever think that. We'll just have to work together to match your symptoms to the right diagnosis and then from there we'll work on a plan to help manage what you're feeling. Does that sound fair?"

Camden looked at me like I was speaking in German. I tried to find the best way in explaining to him that he wasn't "crazy" and validate that his experiences were normal. Other people experienced the same things as he did and he wasn't alone in that sense. I wanted him to know that I was going to be there for him every step of the way as we developed his plan to be able to live his life. I didn't want him to get lost in the darkness. He had one foot in already, and I was there, ready to pull him out. After all, it was my job now, to do what I couldn't do for Kevin.

Much to my mom's dismay, instead of becoming a medical doctor, I became a psychiatrist. I still went to Harvard, but she wouldn't stop talking about her disappointment and that made me happy.

I am still bitter about Kevin deciding that permanently going away was the best solution, but I am bitter for selfish reasons. I wanted my family back. I wanted to have a brother again. I wanted him to be the fun uncle to my children and make cola milk for them. I wanted to start our own traditions with our own families and actually have it be fun. There were so many things I had pictured for the future and now I had to imagine it without him there. If he were here, he'd tell me I was being a brat and I should just get over it.

I didn't want to get over it. I wanted to tell Kevin's story. I wanted to talk about it so that maybe someone would feel comfortable enough to talk about their story as well.

So, I became the help that Kevin needed. I volunteered to be a call center operator for our regional suicide hotline center. When I wasn't doing that, I spoke at mental health conferences and talked about my brother. I spoke at panels where family members would attend to understand how to handle or help their loved ones through their mental health treatment. I told them what we did wrong. I talked about what I learned in from my experience. But everyone's situation was different, even though we were all going through similar experiences. I couldn't exactly tell them what they should do specifically, but I could give them the tools with different options to show their loved one that they really do care and will be there for them.

All the tools that I wish I had when Kevin was going through his daily struggles. I know he wouldn't want me to carry that guilt with me for the rest of my life. But it would always be with me.

I just hope I save enough people's lives to make up for losing Kevin's.

Acknowledgements

First, I'd like to express my gratitude to an amazing author and whom I'm lucky to call my friend, Odessa Rose, for giving me guidance throughout writing this novella. Without her support, I would not have made it this far with the story.

Second, thank you to my sister and fellow writer, Mo Sano, who has inspired me every day to write and tell stories that not everyone would be willing to tell. I'm in awe of your strength, perseverance, and courage. Thank you for helping me with fact checking as I wrote and for being so open with me.

Last, thank you to my husband, Joe, who had to read this novella a dozen times throughout my many edits and revisions. Without your support I wouldn't be able to have the courage to publish.

The list of thanks goes on to the beta readers from the Facebook group, indie authors who answered my many questions, my patrons on Patreon, NaNoWriMo for having a platform to allow me to start writing this story and of course my friends and family who have supported me throughout my writing journey.

About the Author

Emi Sano grew up in a small town of New Hampshire and studied Film at Rochester Institute of Technology where she crafted her storytelling in the form of scriptwriting. Emi has worked in the film industry as a screenwriter and script supervisor. Her writing career took off after she started a writing blog [writingcreatingmagic.com] where she would post short stories.

The stories she writes and chooses to work on are mainly about real life dramas, but she isn't afraid to dabble in fantasy/folklore every now and then.

Emi enjoys her time with her family, whether it is exploring the nature around her in North Carolina or in the comfort of home.

Emi recently published *Voices: a short story collection,* and has more short stories posted on her website.

Follow on Facebook & Instagram:
@emisanowrites